P9-DME-410

Write and Draw your own Comics

This book helps you to...
...create lots of characters
Howdy!
Aaaar!
Hello there!
...think up story ideas
...write dialogue
...use sound effects
GULP!
?
CRACK!
Creak!
...draw action
...and emotion
...and put all that together.
Your hand
This book
Cool

Write and Draw your own Comics

With amazing comic strips by...

Contents

How to use this book 6

Comics: the basics 8

Making up characters 10

Drawing characters 12

Action drawings 14

Speech bubbles 16

Sound effects 18

Once upon a blank 20

Plotting 24

Rough planning 26

Pencils and inks 28

Your own comics 30

Mix and match comic 32

Good day, bad day 38

Superheroes vs robots 44

Dinos in danger 50

Pirates and treasure 56

Tiny adventure 62

Secret agents 68

Fantasy quest 74

How to be a cat 80

Time travel 86

Drawing covers 92

A few last tips 94

How to use this book

Comics use words and pictures to tell stories. This book has lots of space for you to write and draw your own comic strips, but there are also strips that have been drawn already to guide you.

Useful things

Comics: the basics

The stem of a speech bubble points to the speaker.

To keep things looking interesting, comics artists draw their characters from different angles and distances.
You can zoom in really close...

...or zoom out to show more of your characters.
Good! Now you can see me too!

With a wide panel like this, you can show a whole landscape. That's especially useful for setting a scene.
You can also reveal something that has been next to a character all along. Eep!

Not all panels have to be box-shaped.
We're being reflected in the monster's eye!

Try to keep your characters recognizable all the way through a comic.
URGLE?
Suddenly looking completely different is good for hiding from monsters...
... but it's very confusing for everyone else.

Making up characters

Your character

Turn this stick figure into a character by adding clothes and accessories. Fill in the blanks in the thought and speech bubbles, too.

Hello, my name is

.....

and the thing I want most in life is

..... .

One thing no one knows about me is...

.....

..... .

Giving your character a distinctive feature or two means your reader can easily tell that it's the same person all the way through your comic.

Ideas for features and accessories

Drawing characters

In comics, you can draw faces in all sorts of different ways.

Here are a few ways to draw parts of faces.

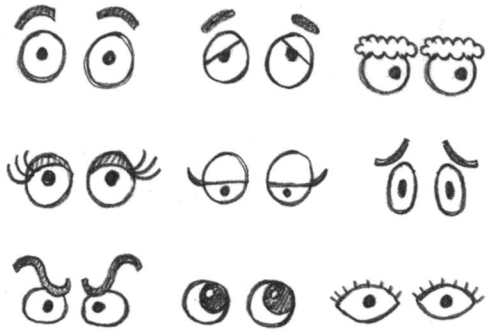

Eyes and eyebrows

Noses

Mouths

Ears

Here are some simple ways to draw facial expressions.

Winking

Happy

Angry

Sad

Scared

Surprised

Laughing

Suspicious

Now try adding expressions and features to these faces to match their names.

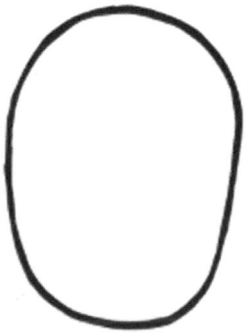

Suzy Brightside

Rocky Hardnut

Baddie McNasty

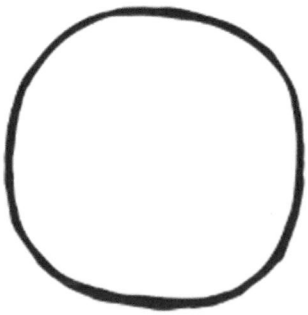

General Temperburst

Characters come in all shapes and sizes.
Here are a few basic body types you can use in your comics.

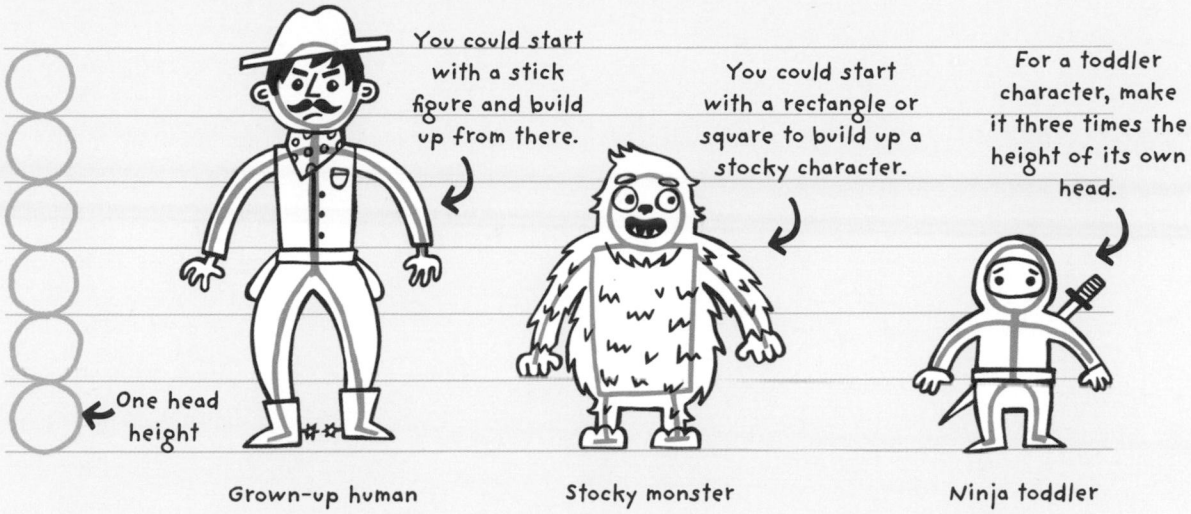

Draw your own characters with different body types. Add some details and facial expressions.

Name: ..... Name: ..... Name: .....

Action drawings

When you're making up characters, try drawing them in lots of different action poses. That helps you get a better feel for how they move around the page.

The little lines next to the figures show movement.

Some action poses to try in your comics

You can spread actions over several panels.
For example, here is a character jumping over an abyss.

Here are some four-legged creatures in action.

Try drawing a four-legged creature in action.

Drawing animals doing human activities can be funny.

Speech bubbles

Comics use speech bubbles – also known as speech balloons – to show that a character is talking.

What do you think these animals are saying?
Add speech bubbles to show their conversation.

Sound effects

Noises in comics are sometimes called sound effects or SFX. The letter shapes used for SFX often reflect the sounds that are being made.

School trip of terror

Use the stickers at the end of this book to add sound effects to this comic.

Once upon a blank

Long ago in a fairy tale kingdom, there was a rabbit prince.
Fill in the blanks in this four-page comic to complete his story.

What are they saying?

Give the characters names.

Draw a magical creature to pull the carriage.

What are the guests at the ball saying and thinking?

Is the fairy king welcoming his guests? Or complaining about the food?

What's on the fairy queen's mind? Is she enjoying herself?

What are the dancing mice talking about?

Write a sound effect for a noise of something scary that's coming to get them.

Try saving up surprises for after a page turn. For example, on this page, there's suddenly a great big... well, that's for you to decide.

Draw what the characters are running away from and add sound effects for the noise it's making.

What does she say in her spell?

What sound does the spell make?

Draw what the fairy godmother has turned the scary thing from the opposite page into.

What does the frog say about the magical transformation?

Plotting

A comic needs a plot – or story – with a beginning, a middle and an end. Here's one way to create a plot.

Finally, show how your character ends up. Happy? Sad?

THE END

Now try writing some notes for a plot of your own.

Your story's title:

Beginning

Your main character is...
(Who? What?)

Your story starts in...
(Place)

The story gets started when...

Middle

One problem your character comes up against is...

Your character reacts by...

There's a surprise when...

End

The character's problems are solved when...

At the end of the comic, your character is....
(Feeling? Doing?)

scribble!

Rough planning

Once you've decided what happens in your comic, decide how many panels you want to use to tell the story. It can be helpful to write a list and sketch out a small, rough version showing what will happen in each panel.

PANEL 1: A knight is riding. A king calls to him for help.

PANEL 2: On the castle roof, the king points out a dragon.

PANEL:3 The knight fights the dragon with his lance.

PANEL 4: The dragon's fire melts the lance.

PANEL 5: The knight pushes the dragon into the river.

PANEL 6: The dragon gives up. Without its fire, it has no power.

Mini, rough comics like this are often called thumbnails.

Title: KNIGHT vs DRAGON

Try drawing your own rough sketches for a comic – perhaps the story you planned on page 25. The sketches can be as messy as you like, and you don't have to use all the panels. Start by jotting down a list on rough paper of what you want to show in each panel.

Title:

Pencils and inks

It's often a good idea to draw your comics in pencil first, then pen. The first half of this comic shows the stages many comic book creators go through.

Pictures and speech bubbles drawn in pencil

Black ink added over pencils

Pencil lines erased

Foreground (the front of the picture) filled in

Background filled in and shading added

Black ink added over the words in speech bubbles

Go over the rest of this strip in black pen. Then fill in the foreground and background in pencils or pens.

Your own comics

(Mix and match comic, pages 33-37)

(Good day, bad day, pages 39-43)

(Superheroes vs robots, pages 46-49)

(Dinos in danger, pages 52-55)

(Pirates and treasure, pages 58-61)

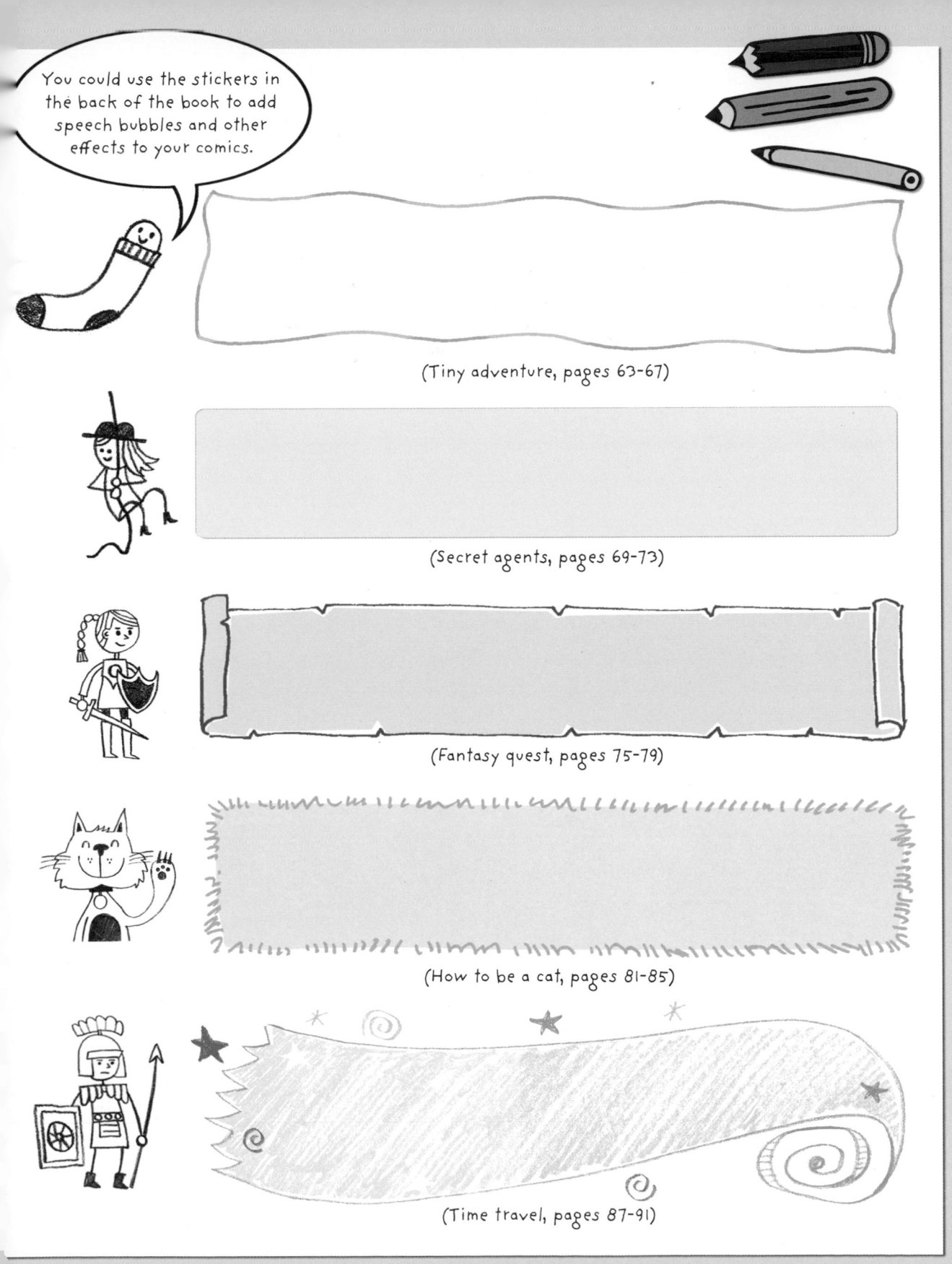
You could use the stickers in the back of the book to add speech bubbles and other effects to your comics.
(Tiny adventure, pages 63-67)
(Secret agents, pages 69-73)
(Fantasy quest, pages 75-79)
(How to be a cat, pages 81-85)
(Time travel, pages 87-91)

Mix and match comic

Choose from these characters and places to create a comic. There are suggestions for events and hints along the way to help you.

Characters

Astronaut on the run from the space police

Pirate mermaid

Bear who's obsessed with watching TV

Excitable robot

Talking skull with a bad attitude

Queen bee

Grumpy circus performer

Mysterious woman on horseback

Annoying little brother or sister

Places

An underground city

Magical library

An alien planet

A park

A supermarket

A spooky forest full of eyes

Fairyland

Ancient Egypt

Now start your comic.

What's your title?

Pick a main character and a place for your story to start.

Show your character going about her or his daily life. You could divide up the panels if you like.

Drawing conversations

Single speaker

Speaker and listener

Two speakers. The first speaker's bubble is higher than the second speaker's.

Continued

A new character arrives. Pick one from the page opposite. What do the two characters say to one another?

Things take a turn for the worse. Pick an event that makes things more difficult for the characters.

Events

A character...

...gets kidnapped.
...is sucked through a portal into another dimension.
...goes to a new school.
...goes on a journey.
...learns to fly.
...meets her or his worst enemy.
...eats or drinks something forbidden.
...flies through an asteroid field.
...climbs a mysterious flight of stairs.
...fights a duel.

Your main character finds an object that helps to make things better.

Objects

Key

Crown

Kitten

Ray gun

Rotten banana

Magic potion

Letter

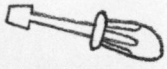
Screwdriver

Your characters go somewhere new.
Pick a place and draw them arriving.

Continued

How do your characters react to the new place?

Screaming

Blushing

Dizzy

Excited

Falling asleep

Something unexpected happens.
(Pick another event.)

Using a huge panel can make a dramatic event seem even more important. You can also show lots of action happening at once.

Something happens to complicate your main character's life.

What does your character do about it?

The end.

(Or is it?)

Endings

Big battle

Party

Goodbye

To be continued...

Good day, bad day

Jot down some good and bad things to happen in your comic.

The events could be realistic or fantastical.

Start your comic on the next page.

What's your title?

Start with either a bad or a good thing happening. Your day could take you anywhere in the world (or out of it).

Vary the scale of the pictures in your panels.

Close up

From a distance

08.00

Continued

Good things

Lottery win

Woohoo!

Discover a new species

Bad things

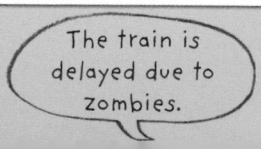

You could use some captions like these to show time passing.

Later...

After lunch...

Meanwhile...

Some time later...

Seconds later...

That evening...

Continued

Good things

Exotic beach trip

Find a chocolate fountain

Meet a helpful person

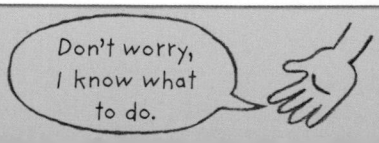

Lose at a computer game

Fall down a hole

Meet a hungry crocodile

The end.

Does your day end with a good thing or a bad thing?

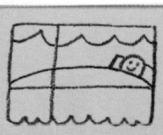

Comfy bed

Something nasty under the bed

Strange noises keeping you awake

Sweet dreams

Superheroes vs robots

In a superhero story, the bad guys have to be extra-powerful, or it would be too easy for your hero to beat them.

Give your superhero a weakness too — perhaps there's something your character is super-allergic to or afraid of.

Before you start...

What's your hero like? Fill in this card.

NAME _____

POWERS _____

_____

WEAKNESSES _____

PERSONALITY _____

Draw your superhero here.

You could include some of these things in your costume design.

Start your comic on the next page.

Step-by-step killer robot

What's your title?

Draw some killer robots rampaging through a city. Then draw your hero arriving in the next panel.

In this big panel, show how your superhero attacks the robots.

You can make your characters look as though they're moving by using lines like these.

Here's a simple way to draw the buildings in the background.

Continued

Does anyone come to help your superhero?

Mayor of Metrotown

WOO-WOO-WOO!!

Innocent bystander

Sidekick

Giant killer robots don't make themselves... who do you think is in control of these metal menaces?

Show your hero facing his or her enemy. What does the villain want?

How does your hero defeat the evil villain and the killer robots?

The end.

How does your superhero feel at the end? Was this an average day or your hero's greatest challenge yet?

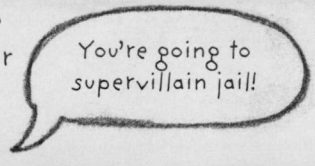

Dinos in danger

Here are some ideas for dinosaurs you could use in your comic. What are their personalities like?

I could be a vicious killer.

But then again, maybe I'm just a great big teddy bear with tiny arms.

Am I cheerful? Nervous? Brave? Talkative? Really, really annoying?

Everyone can see that I'm enormous, but am I good or evil? Brainy or a little slow?

I'm a prehistoric wasp!

BZZZZ!

Am I helpful or harmful? Friend or foe?

Do your dinosaurs work as a team? Do they all like one another? Are some enemies?

Drawing dinos

Flying dinosaur

Large vegetarian dinosaur

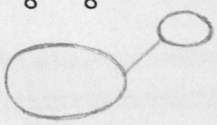

Carnivorous T-rex

Draw your dino character here in an action pose.

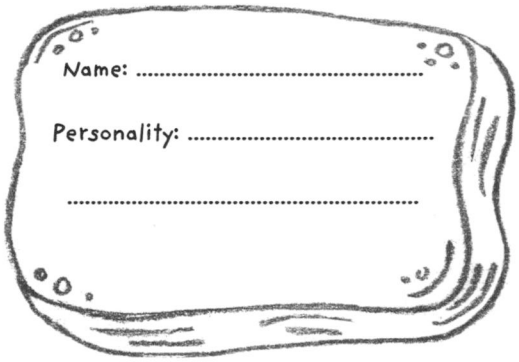

Try drawing a large dinosaur from below to make it look even bigger.

Make a tiny dinosaur appear even smaller by drawing it from above.

Start your dino comic on the next page. →

What's your title?

Dino dangers

Volcanoes

SCREECH!

Rushing, rocky river

Giant insects

Places

COOL CAVE

Drip! Drop! Drip!

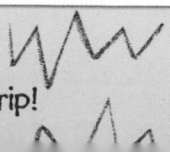

UNDERGROUND LAKE

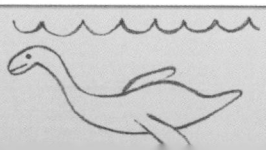

TOWERING MOUNTAIN

WHOOOOOOOOOOOSH!
Meteors
Hidden, hungry things
Rustle
CRACK!
Swish
What was that? It sounded big!
Continued
What shall we do now?
Running away often works.
PUFF! PANT! GASP!
LUSH LEAVES

Dino-hunting Time Tourists

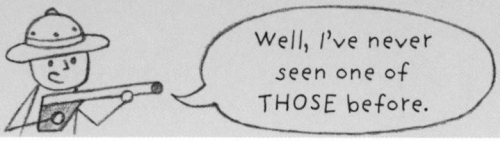

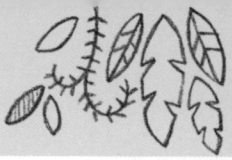

What do the dinos do now? Where do they go?

THICK FOREST

STEAMING SWAMP

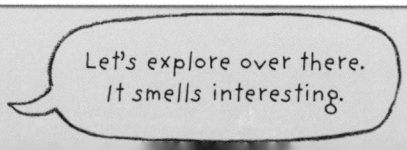

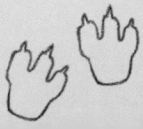

CHITTER

A plague of prehistoric rats

Bigger dinosaurs

Hunger and thirst

The end.

Endings

Find a new home

DEATH

SURVIVAL

Extinct? me? never!

Pirates and treasure

Ahoy there, matey. It be time to make a pirate comic.

Design a pirate

Add a face, hands (or tentacles) and legs (or perhaps a tail) to create your own pirate character.

Is your pirate the captain of a ship? A cabin boy or girl? The ship's cook? A sea monster?

Step-by-step pirate ship

What is your pirate ship's name?

.....

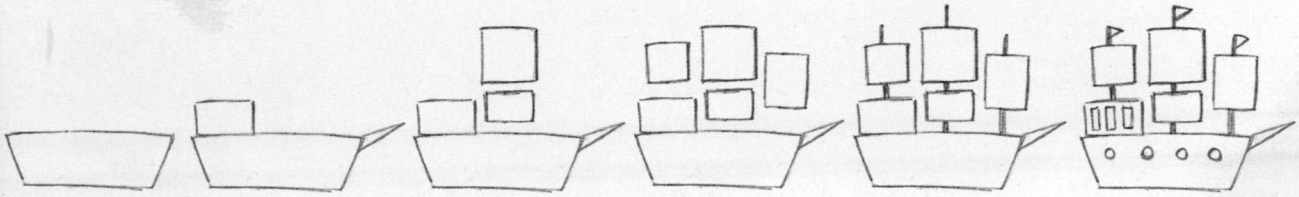

Think up some places your pirates could sail to and add them to this map.

Add an X to mark the spot where the treasure is buried.

Treasure island

Mermaid cove

The sea of lost souls

Add some dangers they might face along the way.

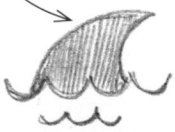

Sharks

Sharp rocks

Terrible storms

Sea monsters

Ghostly pirate ships

Start your pirate comic on the next page. →

AHOY THERE! Lily-livered Scurvy sea dog *Davy Jones's Locker*

What's your title?

Where does your pirate set sail from?

Who's your pirate's crew? Here are some ideas for pirates.

Timmy Tinybones

Captain Plankwalk

Mad Lizzie Tarsniff

Events

Man overboard!

EATEN

Sea battle with enemy pirates

Stock up on supplies

Continued

It's a tough life at sea. Look at all these pirate problems.

Tornado

Tidal wave

Lightning storm

Where is the treasure?

BURIED

SWEAT

What is the treasure?

Gold

Jewels

Worthless old boot

ANGER

GLEE

Does anyone else find the treasure too?

Thieving monkey

Grrr!

The end.

Endings

Huge pirate fight

Swim to safety

Sail home

Retire to a desert island

Share the loot fairly

Tiny adventure

What's your title?

Where do you wake up? Where do you go next?

If you were tiny, sounds would seem louder, so you could use big dramatic SFX letters for what would usually be quiet sounds.

Someone shutting a drawer, maybe.

Continued

Getting around

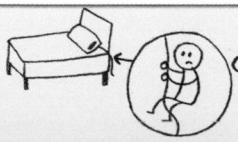

Don't look down, don't look down...

Finally, a door I have a hope of opening. Maybe I can hurl myself through it?

Physical activities

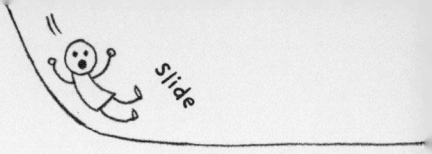

When you're tiny, you have to improvise...

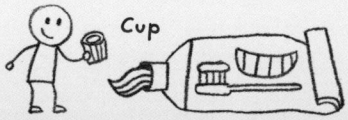

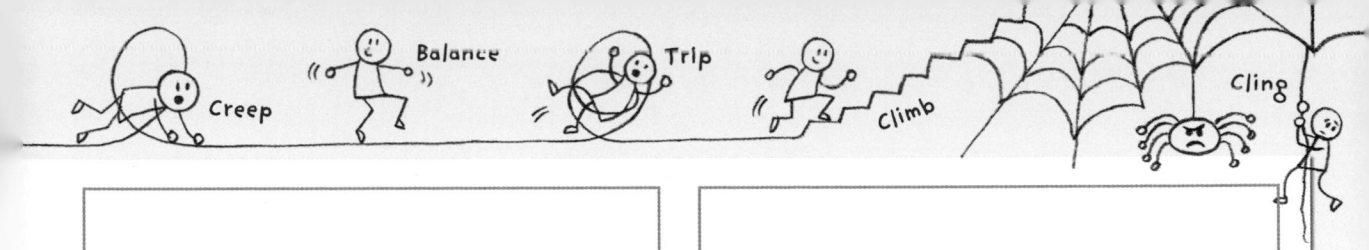

Continued

Tiny person dangers

Mini hiding places

As your story reaches its climax, what if...

...you shrank even more?

...you grew to a giant size?

The end.

Ending ideas

You become ruler of the insects in the park.

You make a snug home in your sock drawer.

You go back to normal and write a comic about your experiences.

Secret agents

Fill in this top secret ID card for your spy character.

Is this a government agency such as MI6 or the CIA? A private company? Aliens?

Real name.....

Cover identity.....

Employer.....

Current mission.....

.....

CLASSIFIED

Start your spy comic on the next page.

Mission ideas

Retrieve a top secret computer file from an enemy base.

Rescue a hostage.

Stop a bomb from going off.

This could be your spy's first mission. Perhaps it's a test to see if she or he will make a good spy?

Continued

Spy words

CLASSIFIED Mystery assailant **ASSASSIN** For Your Eyes Only

Panel ideas

You could just draw a speech bubble against a black background for a panel in darkness.

To show a speaker without revealing her or his identity, try this.

You could draw some panels from the character's point of view, as though looking through their eyes... or their binoculars.

Gadgets and kit

Bug (for listening in to conversations)

Parachute

Disguise

Fake passport

Robot surveillance bee

Handler (a spy's boss)

Tailing (following enemies)

cryptography (code making and breaking)

Biological weapon

Password

Continued

Spy places

Top secret headquarters

Park (a good spy meeting spot)

Dark abandoned garage

TAKA-TAKA-TAKA

BIP BEEP

Spy problems

Gadget malfunction

Traitors and double agents

Car chase

Explosive device

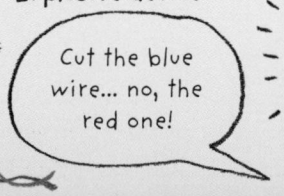

Wrong password

AUTO DESTRUCT MODE INITIATED...

The end.

...REPORTING... MISSION A TOTAL FAILURE/SUCCESS...AGENT STATUS: LIVING/DEAD/DEFECTED TO THE ENEMY...

Fantasy quest

Some fantasy characters you could use

Genie from a magic lamp

Wise old man

Orphaned goblin

SNIFF!

SOB!

Will you be my friend?

Tough unicorn

I will help you fight your enemies.

Evil overlord

MWAHAHAHA!

Sea serpent

Brave dwarf

Weird monster

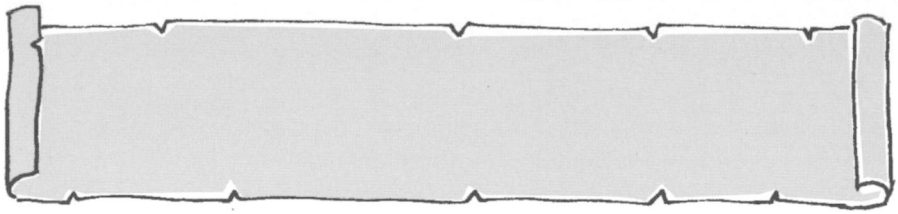

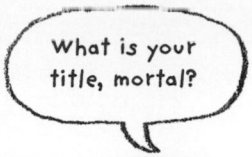

Who or what is your questing hero and what is she or he seeking?

Goblin

Human

Dwarf

Sea serpent (Who says sea serpents can't be heroes?)

Continued

Quest objects

Magic shield that makes you super-strong

Fountain of eternal youth

Sacred chalice of the gods

What terrible and wonderful places does your hero travel through?
Sand dunes
SWELTER!
scorch!

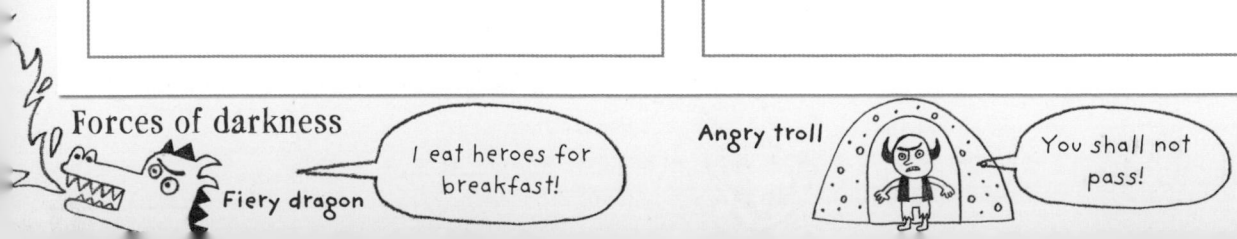
Forces of darkness
Fiery dragon
I eat heroes for breakfast!
Angry troll
You shall not pass!

Is it safe to go in here?
Rushing river
Snowy mountains
Deep, dark caves
Tangled forest
Continued
SNARL!
Giant, poisonous spider
SSSSSSSSSSSS!
Goblin king
Off with their heads! I could use a snack.

Does your hero meet any helpful or friendly characters along the way?

Cuddly giant wolf

Want to ride on my back?

Will the quest succeed?

Magic spell

Just when I thought I was safe...

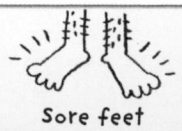

Sore feet

Noble elf (who happens to be quite handy with a bow)

Fun-loving centaur

The end.

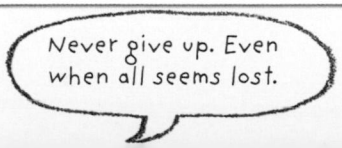

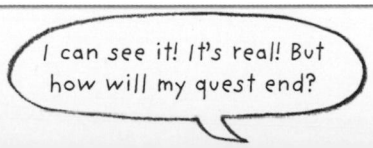

Failure and shame?

Victory and reward?

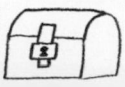

A new quest?

How to be a cat

How does the day start at kitten school?

Some poses

Sitting

Standing

Sleeping

Running

Continued

Kitten faces

Stripes

Smudgy spots

Really big eyes

What are the classrooms like at kitten school?
Do they have any classes outdoors?

Panel ideas

To show the teacher talking to the class, you could draw it like this.

To draw lots of kitties talking together, try this.

If the teacher gets angry and shouts, you could write his or her speech in big letters.

What might make a cat teacher angry?

Watching videos of humans on Mewtube in class

Not sharing your toys

Claiming the dog ate your homework

What experiments might kittens do in a science class?
What songs would they sing in kitten choir?

Continued

What might make a cat teacher happy?

Getting the top grade in a Pouncing exam

Putting your paw up before you meow

A present for teacher

I hope I win the talent show.

Help! There's a dog in the playground!

Yay, school trip!

WOOF!
MRRRRRRROWWWWL!

How does the school day end?
What do the kittens do for fun after school?

The end.

SCRATCH!

MEEP!

PURRRRRRRR!

Time travel

A vessel hurtles through the time stream.
VROOOORP!
VROOOORP!

Decisions, decisions... where and when should the intrepid explorers visit?
CAVE TIMES
ROMAN TIMES
VIKING TIMES
18th CENTURY
19th CENTURY
WORLD WARS
One of these? Or perhaps the future?
Anything but 1482. I'm still not over the food poisoning from last time.

Moments later, the doors slide open.
YEAR:
Draw what's outside the time machine. Where and when has it landed?

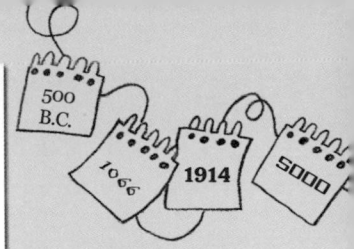

Title?

Who are your time tourists?

Reasons for time travel

To meet famous people?

To change history?

To explore the future?

Continued

Do your characters get into any trouble?
How is life different in the past or future?

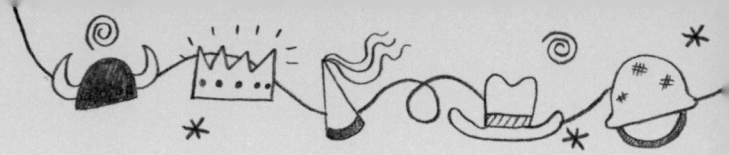

Historical characters

Musketeers

Old-fashioned fighting talk

European royalty

Continued

Ancient Egyptian pharaohs
All must obey me!
Explorers
The Gauls are attacking!
Roman soldiers

Perhaps something goes wrong... your explorers make a mistake, or the time machine breaks?

Time travel trouble

Old-fashioned diseases

Finding yourself in the middle of a brutal war

Time machine breakdown

Oh no! The space-time continuum is broken!

Friends, Romans, Victorians... wait, that's not right!

The end.

Accidentally showing a viking some modern technology

Do the explorers go back to their own time? Or does the journey continue?

Drawing covers

The cover of a comic has to grab your reader's attention and show what the story is about.

Here are a few covers for different types of stories.

The title is usually nice and big – easy to read from a distance.

The title could go on more than one line.

A tag line like this can help lure readers in.

You could draw a very bold cover, without much detail, just shapes and outlines.

Don't forget to leave room for your name somewhere. Comics that are by two people usually just have their last names on the cover.

Draw a cover for one of the comics you've made in this book — or for a comic that you'd love to write one day.

A few last tips

...or talking head comics, that just show characters having a conversation.
I think Sir Galahad has been drawing mean comics about me.
No! How dare he!
Comics can be about anything, from your day at school...
ENTER!
See me in my office
...to a weird dream you had once.
I am the Bermuda Triangle and I will devour you.
Fishsticks! Fishsticks!
And if you ever get stuck...
IN CASE OF BRAIN FREEZE BREAK GLASS.
SMASH!
TINKLE
EMERGENCY COMICS IDEAS
Δ Make a funny comic about a magical creature going to a really normal place such as a grocery store. Does it feel out of place? Or love shopping?
Δ Take a joke you like and turn it into a three-panel comic strip.
Δ Take a simple story you know well and turn it into a comic.
Δ Bring an object to life – a toy, or a household object. What does it do?
Δ Imagine you're a ghost. Who would you haunt?
Δ Think of two fictional characters you love from books, comics or movies. Imagine what would happen if they met.
...try one of these.
Thanks! I'm off to write the tragic tale of a very lonely pencil sharpener.

Who did what in this book?

First published in 2014 by Usborne Publishing Ltd., Usborne House, 83-85 Saffron Hill, London EC1N 8RT, England. www.usborne.com Copyright © 2014 Usborne Publishing Ltd.

All rights reserved. No part of this publication may be reproduced, stored in a retrieval system or transmitted in any form or by any means, electronic, mechanical, photocopying, recording or otherwise, without the prior permission of the publisher. The name Usborne and the devices are Trade Marks of Usborne Publishing Ltd. UE. First published in America in 2015.

Use these stickers on page 19.
GROAN!
CRREAK!
AAAIE!
BONG BONG!
Crunch!
Munch!
AAAH!
SNIFF!
BOOO!
Wooooo
Use the stickers below in your comic strips.

Write in your own words and add these stickers to your comics.

Write in your own words and add these stickers to your comics.

Write in your own words and add these stickers to your comics.